The Mystery Bear

A PURIM STORY

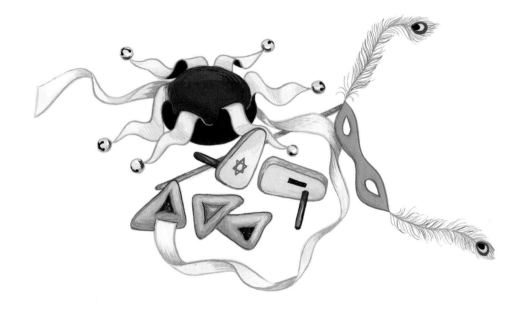

by Leone Adelson

Illustrated by Naomi Howland

CLARION BOOKS

New York

Clarion Books
a Houghton Mifflin Company imprint
215 Park Avenue South, New York, NY 10003
Text copyright © 2004 by Leone Adelson
Illustrations copyright © 2004 by Naomi Howland

The illustrations were executed in gouache on watercolor paper.
The text was set in 12.75-point Leawood Medium.
Book design by Carol Goldenberg.

www.houghtonmifflinbooks.com

Printed in Singapore.

Library of Congress Cataloging-in-Publication Data

Adelson, Leone.
The mystery bear : a Purim story / by Leone Adelson ;
illustrated by Naomi Howland.
p. cm.
Summary: When he awakens from hibernation, Little Bear's hunger leads
him to a house where a Purim celebration is just beginning.
ISBN 0-618-33725-3
[1. Bears—Fiction. 2. Purim—Fiction. 3. Mistaken identity—Fiction.]
I. Howland, Naomi, ill. II. Title.
PZ7.A26My 2004
[E]—dc22   2003012009

ISBN-13: 978-0-618-33725-5
ISBN-10: 0-618-33725-3

TWP   10   9   8   7   6   5   4   3   2   1

With love to my dearest friend and fellow writer,

LILIAN MOORE REAVIN

—L.A.

For ALYCE *and* DOT,
remarkable women and mothers

—N.P.H.

SOMETHING WOKE LITTLE BEAR from his winter sleep. It wasn't his mother. She was still fast asleep. What was it?

His stomach rumbled, as though to say, "I did! I did!"

That was it—Little Bear was hungry. He hadn't eaten anything since last fall, and here it was nearly spring. No wonder he was hungry!

He stuck his head out of the den. Yes, it *was* spring. The snow was almost gone. There must be something out there for a winter-hungry bear to eat.

Little Bear's shaggy head swung this way, that way—looking. His black nose twitched this way, that way—sniffing.

Good news from his nose—a smoke smell. Little Bear didn't know much about the world, but he did know that where there was smoke, there might be cooking. Where there was cooking, there was food, and that's where Little Bear wanted to be.

As fast as he could put one furry foot in front of the other, off he went, sniffing all the way. And there it was! The delicious smell was coming from the chimney of a little house by the river.

The front door of the house was open, and Little Bear could see people inside. The grownups were taking food from the stove to the table. The children were leaping around and tooting horns and shaking wooden rattles. What a frightening noise they made!

Little Bear hid behind a tree, watching, and tried to decide what to do.

His feet said, "Run away."

His nose said, "Stay."

His stomach said, "I'm hungry!"

Run away? Stay? Stay? Run away?

Suddenly, through the woods came a crowd of people.
They were singing and playing music and beating drums.
They wore masks and crowns and beards and false
noses. One was even wearing a whole horse's head.

But Little Bear had eyes only for what they were carrying. Such good things—fruit and nuts and honey. Little Bear's mouth watered.

Honey! To a hungry bear, honey is better than money.

Little Bear came up behind the parade of masqueraders and followed it to the open door. No one stopped him. No one thought he looked strange. After all, it was Purim, and at Purim people dress as they like. Little Bear stood up on his haunches and peered into the house.

The father of the family saw Little Bear and took him by his paw. "Don't just stand there dressed up in your wonderful bear suit," he cried. "Come in, come in, whoever you are! Eat! Drink! It's Purim!"

Little Bear wasted no time. First he took a pawful of honey. Then a swallow of apple juice to wash it down. Then a pawful of raisins, followed by another swallow of apple juice. Then a delicious hamantasch . . .

With all the food and the drink and the noise, he began to feel a bit dizzy.

"Who is that dressed up in the bear costume?" someone
wanted to know.

"If he wasn't so short, I'd say it was Bela the tailor" was
the reply. "Bela makes wonderful suits. See how it fits
him—not a wrinkle."

"No, no, no—it's Peshel the pickle seller," said another. "She always has the best Purim costume."

"It's Heshel the herring man. I'd know his bandy legs anywhere," someone else said. "Hey, Heshel," and the man gave Little Bear a nudge to get his attention.

"You don't have any noisemakers," the man went on. "Here, you can have one of mine." He put a cap with bells on Little Bear's head.

Little Bear looked up from the feast and gave a tiny growl.

Itzik heard it and tugged at his mother's skirt. "Mama," he whispered, "I think it's a real bear."

His mother laughed. "A real bear? In Dovid's house? Drinking juice, eating hamantaschen? Don't be silly, my son."

The leader of the masqueraders stood up on a chair. "Listen, everyone," he cried. "It's time for the Purim play. Where's Queen Esther? And King Ahasuerus? And Mordecai—where are you? Stand here with your horse. And all you people of Persia, gather around. That's it. Now, where's Haman?"

As always on Purim, at the word "Haman" such a booing and horn-blowing and drum-beating broke out that the little house shook and the dishes on the table jumped.

The noise was too much for Little Bear. He sank into a big comfortable chair and closed his eyes. All he wanted was to be left alone.

"Everyone must be part of the Purim spiel," called the leader. "You, too, Bela-Heshel-Peshel, whoever you are. You have to be one of the Persians, too. Come on."

But Little Bear could hardly move. He was too full of good things, and he was very, very sleepy. Never before had he gotten up as early as he had that morning. So he stayed where he was.

The people shouted in his ear, they shook him, and they tickled him. Little Bear gave a tiny growl.

Only Itzik heard it. He tugged at his mother's sleeve. "Don't touch him. He's a real bear—I just know it," he whispered.

But no one paid any attention to Itzik.

"Wake up, wake up!" they shouted at the mystery bear. "It's time for the Purim play!" Someone poked Little Bear with a stick.

The point of the stick landed right in the middle of Little Bear's full belly. He gave a tiny grunt. Itzik heard that, too.

Itzik tugged harder at his mother's skirt. "Mama!" he whispered. "Don't touch him! He's a real bear, I tell you."

But his mother did not hear him. She gave Little Bear a shake to wake him up.

That was too much for Little Bear. He leaped out of the chair with a roar. His white teeth flashed, and his mouth opened wide to show his great red tongue.

All the Purim players shrank back in fear. "It's a bear!" they cried. "It's a real bear! Run for your lives!"

The people tumbled out of the house and ran to hide.
They hid in barrels. They climbed trees. They scrambled
onto rooftops. They crowded into the cowshed and hid
behind the cows. Some even jumped into the river.

But Little Bear did not chase them. Why should he? He'd had all he could eat and drink. All he wanted now was to go back to his den and finish his winter sleep.

He started toward the woods, but for some reason he could not stay on the path. Little Bear was too sleepy and too full of food.

Itzik and his mother came out from behind the haystack where they'd been hiding and watched Little Bear disappear among the trees.

"I tried to tell you, Mama!" said Itzik. "I tried to tell you he was a real bear."

"And you were right," said his mother. "What a smart son I have!" She gave him a hug.

Little Bear crept into his den. There lay his mother, still fast
asleep. Little Bear snuggled as close to her as he could. She
threw a great paw around him. He gave a deep, deep sigh, and
soon both of them were finishing their long, long winter sleep.

A Note

PURIM IS A DAY of feasting and rejoicing to celebrate the deliverance of the Jews from a massacre. It is observed on the fourteenth day of Adar, the sixth month in the Jewish calendar, which falls between late February and the middle of March.

The story in the biblical Book of Esther (also called the Megillah) tells of Ahasuerus, king of Persia, and his queen, Esther, who was Jewish. An important official named Haman hated the Jews—especially Esther's uncle, Mordecai, who refused to bow down to him. Haman decided to have all the Jews killed, and he chose the day for this event by casting lots with small stones, which was one of the ways people made decisions in ancient times. The name of the holiday comes from the Hebrew word *pur,* which means "lots." Purim is also called the Feast of Lots.

When he learned about Haman's plan, Mordecai asked Queen Esther for help. She told King Ahasuerus that Haman was sending soldiers to kill the Jews and that the Jewish people should be allowed to take up arms and defend themselves, which ordinarily they were forbidden to do. King Ahasuerus granted this request, and also decreed that Haman's punishment would be death.

On Purim the Megillah is read in synagogues, and noisemakers called *gragers* are shaken whenever Haman's name is mentioned. A festive meal is prepared that includes hamantaschen, triangular pastries shaped to resemble Haman's three-cornered hat and filled with poppy seeds and honey, apricots, or prunes. Young and old traditionally dress up in costumes and perform a Purim play, or Purim spiel, acting out the story of Esther. On this joyful day, the Jewish people are happy to recall Queen Esther and to celebrate their survival despite this particular Haman and others who followed him.